TO HEAVEN

TO HEAVEN

Gill Noffort

The story, all names, characters, and incidents portrayed in this production are fictitious. No identification with places, buildings, and products is intended or should be inferred.

For information about special discounts for bulk purchases or to book an event with our author(s), please contact EFM Management at www.efm-management.com.

Paperback ISBN: 979-8-218-94678-4

Book Cover by Vikki

First Edition

To E.N., the light that never wavers

SAMUEL comes home, and dinner is almost on the table. He sighs as he pushes back the curtain in the entryway and drops his day's pay on the floor in the entryway. He waits to scoop up little Naomi, who runs from the kitchen to meet him in the doorway. He spins her around a few times while he carries her back into the kitchen. Naomi smiles wide-eyed at her father as she's spun around in his calloused hands. Samuel drops her in her seat at the kitchen table and moves to kiss his wife, Zahava, who stands over the fire tending to a small fish, soon to be laid on the bed of lentils that sit on the table. Zahava smiles upon receiving her husband's affections, but as the kiss breaks, her expression turns to one of concern. Naomi grasps at the dish in front of her as Samuel laughs and sneaks her some lentils from the plate. He walks to the door and picks up his wages.

One daric, split into twenty silver shekels sits in the bag. Samuel hands the bag to Zahava. She opens it, and both of them look into the bag.

Zahava inhales sharply, and her expression shifts from concern to worry. "That's barely enough for tax!" she exclaims. "What will the collector say?"

"The same thing he says every month. We will figure this out, Zahava," says Samuel, not only reassuring Zahava, but himself, too. Zahava says nothing, but her gaze says *I hope so.*

"How did it go today?" asks Zahava, after a beat of silence, turning back to the fish. She removes the fish from the fire and sets it upon the lentils.

"We finally finished that tier. They're starting to plan another one tonight. I'm grateful we finished it. The supervisor wasn't happy with our pace on it. I was starting to worry that he'd reduce our wages," says Samuel. Zahava pauses but takes her seat at the table.

"I'm glad you got it done before that happened," she says stiffly, but her voice holds a glimmer of relief. The family eats in silence, only interrupted by Naomi's babbling.

Just after sunrise, Samuel and his co-masons gather at the far side of the site to examine the draft of the next tier of the tower that was planned by the night's crew. Near them, one set of men cut blocks of clay on hods into bricks, and a different set of men unload the hods of wet clay onto a large woven mat in the sun to dry. A third set of men load the dry clay from the mat into blazing kilns lined up in rows. Oxen and mules pulling carts of bricks trot around the site, delivering hods of bricks to the tower from the kilns and back again, their carts empty. Hods on hoists scale the tower, zipping up and down as a man at the base pulls the rope which controls the hoist. Everything works in synecdoche, and the masons take their place in the rhythm of work.

"Ten feet in from the previous tier each way, up for forty more layers! Keep the stairs going with you!" yells the supervisor.

"Hand me that," says Samuel, atop the new tier, pointing to a tapered metal object lying near him. Once it is in his hand, he takes a trowel full of the viscous gypsum substance out of the bucket to his left and places it on top of the previous layer of bricks. He takes some bricks from the hod before him and lays them on top of the mortar. His coworker, Daryush, scrapes the excess mortar from the bricks and back into the bucket. They repeat this process late into the day, until Daryush and Samuel's tunics are both soaked with sweat. The sun beats down hot on the working men, but they persist.

"Let's pick up the pace, boys!" yells the supervisor. "We need this tower to ascend to heaven!"

"To heaven!" yell the crowd of workers, before returning to work.

Streaks of sweat run off Samuel's face and onto the brick. He watches the drops of sweat fall from his hairline, and he wonders if he's physically capable of working any faster. He slicks his hair back and slaps another trowel full of mortar onto the preceding layer of bricks and smooths it out. He pants as he grabs another brick and places it in the mortar. Daryush scrapes off the excess, complaining that his knees hurt. Samuel's knees hurt too, but the only way to get through the day is to ignore the pain. Only when the water clock sinks two more times can Samuel return to his family. As the day proceeds, it gets harder to focus on the work: all that he could think about at the moment was bathing at the hammam, dinner, and sleep, but at least the tower was getting somewhere. At the end of the day, They do not finish the tier that they had started, but the expectation that they would is unrealistic. Samuel's entire body aches. His shoulders hang low and he only saunters to the supervisor to collect his day's pay—twenty more shekels—and begins the walk home.

He mopes through the city, thinking about how he will possibly gather the energy to stabilize the arches tomorrow with Daryush, and how he'll possibly acquire enough to pay the tax collector, especially when the day's pay is always under threat of changing. It's fulfilling, being a part of something greater than oneself, even with all of the obstacles that come with such a task. He looks towards the mountains ahead of him, far in the distance, eyeing wistfully the homes near the bathhouse that he could only dream of affording. When the tower is finished, it will be he, Zahava, and Naomi living in those houses. Samuel will never have to touch a brick again. By that day, all of the labour, the hours, the pain will have been worth it.

Just then, low to the ground, yet above Samuel's head flies a great, dark eagle. Its wingspan is almost wide enough to trap itself between the buildings on each side of the road. He pauses, awestruck, as the eagle glides, weaving through the tops of the buildings. Everyone else on the road steers around him as he stands. The city-folk drift in and out of the shops lining the road, calling to their companions. A goat bleats, tied to a fencepost. Children run through the streets, chased by their parents. A woman shouts from her balcony. Amidst the bustle of the city center, Samuel's neck remains craned to the skies, commanded by the bird. He almost wishes he could be the bird. How easy it would make things—to be unburdened, to fly. Perhaps, thinks Samuel, there is still something that ties the bird down. Perhaps it is a mother or father on the lookout for food. Or it's scouting for a place to build a grand nest that is so typical of eagles. The bird flies away as quickly as it had come, and Samuel's eyes follow it to the distance for just a moment longer before returning to his thoughts.

The tax collector is supposed to come two days from now, and Samuel and his family barely have enough for meat and grain, let alone tax. His body tense and sore, he walks into his home and scoops up little Naomi, just like always. She squeals with joy upon being lifted and spun around, and then dropped back at the table. Zahava stops her cooking upon her husband's entrance and pauses. She takes his face in her hands. His skin is dry to the touch, and his beard is overgrown. He relaxes in his wife's hands.

"Samuel, you're working yourself to death," says Zahava.

"We need to eat somehow," sighs Samuel. Looking into the bright, dark eyes of his wife and daughter, he is reminded why he does it all. He smiles.

The meal on the table is considerably smaller than last night's, two small filets of fish over a barley porridge.

"Both of you, eat," says Zahava. "I'm not hungry." She serves Samuel and Naomi each an appropriate portion, and the serving plate is clean. Her stomach growls.

"Zahava, please," Samuel urges, pushing his serving towards her.

She shakes her head and holds her hands out in front of her. "I said I'm not hungry." This time, her stomach does not betray her.

"You can't just sit here and starve and worry yourself to death," says Samuel. Naomi lifts her head from eating and looks at both her parents. Her lip quivers. The fish and lentils steam from the table, the earthy smell wafts through the air, yet no one touches the plate.

"It's not something I can run from. I'm around it all day."

"So am I. You think I don't think about this? I'm supposed to be providing for us and I can't do that! Do you think that the guilt doesn't eat at me each day?"

Zahava turns her head away and looks at the ground. She says nothing. Samuel inches the plate towards Zahava's end of the table.

"It's okay, mama," says Naomi, trying to comfort her mother.

Both parents smile at Naomi's assurance. Zahava looks at the plate before her and begrudgingly starts eating from it.

"I'll have to start working nights, too."

"Samuel—"

"There's no other way," he says. "The tax collector comes the day after tomorrow, and we don't even have enough to eat."

"I could sell cloth in the bazaar," she suggests, but Samuel looks at her confused.

"You said that there's no other way but to work nights. There must be something for me to do. I can't stand by and watch you kill yourself," says Zahava. Samuel looks at the loom in the next room over. A piece of cloth, half-finished, lay in it. It's taken Zahava the entirety of three afternoons to make this much progress.

"I'll be here a long time, Zahava. I'm not killing myself over this," says Samuel.

"You will, if you give your food to me, and go back to the site on an empty stomach. Look at you! Tense, gaunt, exhausted. This isn't healthy and we can't live like this forever," retorts Zahava. She inhales sharply, almost gasping with her mouth closed, after she finishes speaking.

"I'm sorry, Samuel, I—"

Samuel shakes his head, cutting her off."I don't think we have another choice," he admits

"Not if you won't let me help you."

Samuel sighs."It isn't you, love, it's—" he pauses and looks at the loom in the next room again. "Half of that cloth took you three days to make, and you'll only be paid a fraction of what I make in a day. It just is not worth the labour. By the time you've finished with that cloth over there," he points to the loom, "The tax collector will have come and gone."

"At least I won't work myself sore and sick like a dog," says Zahava.

"For you all, I'd do it three times over." Zahava looks at the ceiling, and then at the ground.

"I know, but—"

Naomi's voice cuts the tension as she announces that she has finished her meal. The fire in Zahava's eyes dissipates, as both look at Naomi.

"I guess you're right," says Zahava, watching Naomi, who pounds her fist on the table. "I need to be here, for her."

Samuel smiles, sadly, wishing he could do the same.

Anything for little Naomi.

The following morning, Samuel wakes up just before dawn to find his wife still sound asleep. In the morning, she will go to the bazaar and buy the cheapest cut of fish and lentils that she can find. It will go to Naomi. Hunger born of love is pain worth taking, just like the soreness, the sunburns, the long hours away. Samuel begins the walk to work already prepared to get the day's shift over with and begin the night's. He still enjoys the monotony of his task: lay mortar, lay bricks from the hod atop that, and then Daryush or some other coworker will smooth off the sides. Repeat this task until the water clock has sunk and replenished eight times, the supervisor inevitably yells at you, or you finish a tier and must start anew.

"Let's go, boys! We haven't got all eternity!" yells the supervisor, walking up the tower and surveying.

"Looking good! Let's keep it up," he booms at Samuel and Daryush, finishing another arch, while a third mason mixes mortar. Supporting the arch with one hand while the mortar dries, Samuel flashes his boss a sheepish yet proud smile, pushing his hair out of his face and fanning himself with his tunic.

Late into the night, when many of the other men had already gone home to their wives and children, and the day supervisor traded with the night's, the men finally finish the next tier.

There is dirt all over Samuel's body. His thighs and shoulders burn so much that they sting. The men stand back, examining their work, huffing and puffing. But there is no time for breaks. One tier is finished, and it is immediately time to start the next one.

The men gather near the hods. Fresh-cut brick dries slowly in the moonlight. The kilns roar and crackle, their blaze incessant. The supervisor's supervisor lays in front of the crew a large clay tablet, depicting the plans for the next tier of the tower. From the top view, three rings are etched into the clay, inside of a fourth circle, the base of the tower. The outermost ring of the base holds decorative arches, and stairs scale the wall behind them. On the other face of the wall are plans for family homes within the tower. As the tower starts to gain more height, some of the masons, by themselves or with their families, are moving into the tower to live. The men examine the draft before them and divide the work between them until the early morning hours. They don't even lay down any bricks. By the end of the night shift, Samuel has four hours to go to the hammam and return home to sleep. He takes his combined pay– two darics, forty shekels, and starts for the bathhouse.

He comes home wet from the hammam and sets his earnings down on the table in the kitchen and walks toward the bedroom. He enters the room to see Naomi thrashing in her sleep. Zahava sits awake in their bed. The circles under her eyes look darker since yesterday.

"Why are you awake?" he asks.

Zahava shrugs, "I couldn't sleep. I've been awake for most of the night. I turn to one side and try to fall asleep, and then I turn to the other. Then I lay on my back. No reprieve anywhere."

Samuel cocks his head to the side and passes a sympathetic look towards Zahava.

` "Why not?" he says, pretending that he doesn't know. Zahava looks to the ceiling, like she's trying to find a hidden shape in the stucco.

"You know why," she says, after pausing for a moment. "I was worried about you, about—" she gestures above her "—this."

"Don't worry about me. You need to get out of your own head." Samuel takes Zahava's hand in his and helps her out of bed. Together, they walk from the bedroom through the atrium into the kitchen. Samuel opens his bag of wages and he and Zahava look into the bag. The wages from the past two days make enough for tax and a small dinner.

Zahava smiles softly as she looks into the bag—A fleeting solace. She turns to look at Samuel. His face is gaunt, and his shoulders hang lower than they did three days ago.

"Samuel, I'm serious. You're going to work yourself sick."

"I can hold out, I'll be fine," he says, trying to convince Zahava and himself. "There's not any other option. This tower must reach heaven. Then all of this work will be worth it. Once it's finished, they will pay each of us sums of money only seen by the king himself. I'll never have to touch a brick, a stone, a trowel again."

Zahava looks through the atrium to the sky, her expression concentrated and hopeful, but there is an unshaking skepticism in her eyes as Samuel speaks. Another great eagle flies above the house. The clouds obscure and expose the moon and stars as the bird flies in the opposite direction of the clouds. Zahava's gaze remains tethered to the bird as she watches it glide.

"Look at that bird," she says. "I've never seen anything like it."

Samuel's eyes follow hers. "I saw one just like it the other day. It almost trapped itself between two of the homes near the hammam. I stopped in the middle of the street just to watch it go."

"I wish I could pet it, it must be soft," says Zahava.

Samuel disappears into the bedroom for a moment, and emerges with another bag of money. He places the wages from the past day and night into the bag.

"Give this to the tax collector," he instructs, handing the bag to Zahava. "There are still fifteen in the savings bag, for dinner. Eat well tonight. The sun is rising, I have to go," and he laces up his sandals.

“At least come home for dinner,” pleads Zahava as he walks out the door.

“You know I can’t.”

“Another night?” asks Zahava. “Naomi wouldn’t sleep either, until late into the night last night.”

Samuel sighs in surrender and looks at his daughter. “Just for tonight.” And he walks out the door.

The sun is at zenith and Samuel and Daryush sit on the ledge of the tower eating their lunch, a meager serving of bread and stew. It’s scentless and bland to the taste, but it’s sustenance. The shadow of the tower stretches far in front of them, almost to the edge of the construction site. Daryush looks as worse for wear as Samuel. His hair is dirty and he is sunburnt. His skin is bruised, dark and purple. The lines in his face are more pronounced than they were yesterday, and he is walking ever slower. He takes a bite of bread and stares into the gap between the two of them and infinity. He says nothing for a long time.

“Do you ever think we will finish that tower?” asks Daryush.

“Well, we have to, do we not?” replies Samuel. “It’s how we keep our families alive.”

Daryush shrugs, not agreeing nor disagreeing. An awkwardness hangs in the air, thick like cotton. The two finish their lunch in silence and then return to their work. They say but very few words to each other the rest of the day.

That night, Samuel comes home to his wife and daughter, and he does not eat. Tomorrow, all three of them will. The little victories are celebrated when they can be. He knows that in the morning, he will depart, and only sec his family for a few short hours, and then repeat the process until the tower is done. He does not fall asleep for a long time, he just lays awake, basking in the sight of those he loves. When he does, he falls asleep soundly. Secure, if just for one night. And before the sun rises, he is gone again.

Day after day the men build layer after layer on the tower, and still never can close the gap between them and the aether. The farther up they build, the farther the heavens run. Samuel seems like he would fall into the bucket of mortar face-first at any moment. His hands have gone from calloused to blistered and bloody; he burns with soreness as oxen with cargo. The dark circles under his gentle eyes are darker yet, from many a sleepless night. But each day and each night, he builds ever on. It is all he can do. Finally, the men finish another layer on the tower, but it's not enough for the supervisor, nagging them to move quicker. The tower is thirty-nine stories high, and still has not reached heaven.

"Do you ever think we will finish that tower?" asks Daryush again one night, as he looked into the cosmos.

"Of course. I have to keep the faith. It's hard to hold onto, at some points, but the prize at the end keeps me going."

Daryush exhales from his nose, as if to stifle a laugh.

"What?" asks Samuel, confused. "When the work is done, I'll never have to watch my family starve again. None of us on this crew will have to lie awake at night feeling helpless or hungry or sick. We will touch the sky with the tower's highest spire, all of us".

Daryush shakes his head. "You've always been a faithful man," he says.

In the small hours of the morning, when the moon is still high, Samuel departs with his pay for the hammam. After changing into a bathrobe, he enters the frigidarium. The room echoes with the voices of the other bathers as they converse with one another, gossipping about their day, their problems, their wives. Samuel recognizes some of them as fellow night crew members. Casting his robe aside, he steps into the pool and tenses from the cold water touching his skin. He relaxes, and wades in the pool, finally allowing relaxation to overtake him. He sits there for fifteen minutes, maybe more, entertained by the conversation around him as he lets the frigid water loosen his body roped with muscle. When he emerges, his legs shake for a moment as he adjusts to the air in the room. He grabs his robe and moves into the caldarium, where it is much quieter than the other room. Still wet from the previous bath, he descends the stairs into the pool, tensing and releasing again from the scalding hot water and walks deeper into the pool. He scoops up some water and begins to wash. As he washes, he looks to the skylight. Tonight, the skies are clear, and the stars twinkle in the haze of steam against the backdrop of night.

Since he started to work nights, Samuel enjoyed tracking the constellations as he worked, counting how many he can find and watching them move slightly day by day. It fills his heart to know that people before him found pictures in nature and attached stories to them. It grants a feeling of significance to look up at them: Just like the stars and their stories, the tower will live on—past Samuel, past Naomi, and then some. As he gazes at the stars, another eagle in flight intercepts his view. It is bigger and darker than any of the others he's seen before. It blocks out the light of the moon for a moment as it flies directly over the atrium in the caldarium. Everything turns black around the bathhouse, except for the silhouette of the eagle, illuminated around the edges. At that moment, it looks close enough to snatch out of the air. On an instinct, Samuel reaches his arm above his head. His fingers close into a fist, but he only catches steam in his hand. He can see his thighs below him again; the tiles on the walls glimmer in the moonlight. The eagle above flies on, past the hammam and over the rest of the city.

Samuel's arm stays in the air, frozen, He gazes around the caldarium and sees no one else. Through the steam, the walls seem so high, and the floor so wide. Someone's feet slap against wet tile in the hallway behind him. The drains slosh with water. Samuel closes in upon himself, falling to his knees in the pool. He has long finished washing by this point, but he stays, his gaze returning to the sky. The sensation of smallness he felt in looking around the room only intensifies as he stares up into space. He rises, reaching his hand up again, as if it could ascend through the hole in the ceiling and find an end to the sky, but he can't even reach the ceiling. After all of this time admiring the stars and tracking their constellations, only now does he realize how vast the aether truly is. There must have been a million miles between him and those stars. Perhaps Daryush was right, they never are going to finish that tower.

Samuel exits the pool and grabs a towel. He sits on the bench against the wall. His muscles tighten, cold. The towel around his shoulders, he sits, staring at the ground, unthinking. Footsteps come and go; the booming voices of the men carry through the halls as they enter the caldarium. They look at Samuel, giving him quick acknowledgement, but no one says anything. Samuel takes his time redressing, in slow, controlled motions.

Ascending to the surface from the stairs of the hammam, he thinks about the first time he saw the eagle, how it came so close to trapping itself between those two buildings. He remembers musing about how awesome it would be to become a bird. Now, he feels like putting his foot in his mouth, and somewhat like throwing up. Maybe in some other timeline, the bird really did get stuck. How cruel, a stuck bird.

All of this time, thinks Samuel on the walk through the city, infinity was so tangible. He and his co-masons were the agents of a dream, their families its beneficiaries. He feels the hot sting of tears welling up in his eyes, and looks towards the sky to stifle them. How could he have been so foolish, to think that that tower would actually ascend all the way to heaven? Not to just touch the clouds, but sunder them. Behind him, the tower looms, high above the rest of the city. Not yet sundering the clouds, but dwarfing the other buildings in its wake, blocking out the light of the stars. Earlier in the night he realized how vast the sky was, and now he feels its whole weight. He doesn't dare turn back and look at the tower. Heaven is dual, he realizes: a beacon, but even the light of a beacon has a vanishing point.

What is to do? he thinks. He has a family to feed, but he can barely do that. Time slows as Samuel tries to stop his crying on the walk home. The city center blurs through tears, becoming a chorus of colours and shapes.

He walks into the bedroom to find Zahava and Naomi asleep. He crawls into bed next to Zahava, and sits upright next to her. Silent sobs interrupt her snores as Samuel catches tears in his hands. The minutes feel more like hours, but soon enough, again, it is just before dawn, time to depart. Another day chasing infinity. He struggles to get out of bed, and is slow to dress and lace up his sandals once he rises. He lingers in the room for a few extra seconds before kissing his wife and daughter goodbye, and he walks out the door.

When he arrives at the construction site, an unusual din pervades the place. Usually, people converse amongst themselves as they work, but the tasks of the day take the form of a quiet rhythm perpetually continued. Today, though, no one is laying any bricks, loading any kilns, or mixing any mortar. Instead, everyone darts around the site, up, down, and around the tower in a frantic haze.

When Samuel enters the site at the far end, Daryush walks up and greets him, just like every day. Samuel stares at Daryush with one eyebrow raised for a moment. He understood the intent of what Daryush was saying, but not the words themselves. The words he spoke are nothing similar to the syllables they had shared all this time. Samuel returns the greeting, but is met with the same confusion from Daryush. What had happened, he wonders. Am I going crazy? Samuel attempts to continue his conversation, but Daryush's expression never wavers; he doesn't seem to understand. Samuel pats Daryush on the shoulder and dismisses himself with a wave of his hand. He walks onward past Daryush, looking for the supervisor.

As he walks, a group of the men who work the kilns scream at each other, growing louder with each bout of noises. Each of the men wear confused and frustrated looks on their faces. Samuel stands and watches them for a moment, noticing that no one's making the same noises. Maybe I'm not going crazy, he thinks. Two men near him sit, conversing as normal, but no one else seems to be able to do the same. He looks to the hoists, trying to find men or bricks scaling the tower, yet the hoists are empty and unmoving. Oxen buck, breaking the yokes that hold them. A boy of about fifteen runs after them, calmly speaking to the poor animals, but in a different set of noises than the ones the kiln men made. The supervisor gestures at the men in front of him with wild, grand motions. He swings his arms above his head, pointing left and right.

Samuel stares, dumbfounded and confused. He tilts his head, listening deeply into the din. The voices layer on top of each other until it dawns on him that there is a sense to all the screaming: there is a set pattern to the sounds that everyone is making, and everyone makes different ones— words, perhaps? He wonders what could have happened here in the hours between leaving the site and returning. Seemingly overnight, everyone on the crew had lost the ability to communicate with one another. It's a twisted joke, with a cruelty that only the divine can muster, he thinks. The day after he loses all faith in the completion of this project, no one can see a way to continue. He looks around at the chaos surrounding him, and then up into the distance, past the last layer of the tower, and through the wispy clouds.

Now, the tower in Babylon will never reach heaven.

Other Publications By

Gill Noffert

"blah blah blah" and "With the Wind"
Blue Marble Review

ACKNOWLEDGEMENTS

Thanks to Onyinye Ihezukwu for her infallible belief in Samuel, Zahava, and Naomi. Without her, this story would not exist.

Thanks to the 2024 Introduction to Creative Writing cohort, Earlham College.Your feedback was essential in the development of this story.

Thanks to Demetrios Michaelides and the Classical Studies staff at the University of Cyprus. His articles have been integral to the development of the world of Babylon in which Samuel and his family live.

Finally, thanks to Drew King for alpha reading, and showing me that sometimes your subconscious gets ahead of you.

www.ingramcontent.com/pod-product-compliance
Lightning Source LLC
LaVergne TN
LVHW050612100826
845148LV00015B/3233

9798218946784